MULGA BILL'S BICYCLE

Poem by

A. B. PATERSON

Illustrated by

KILMENY & DEBORAH NILAND

Angus&Robertson
An imprint of HarperCollins*Publishers*

Angus&Robertson

An imprint of HarperCollins*Publishers*, Australia

First published in Australia in 1973 by William Collins Pty Ltd
First published in paperback in 1976
Reprinted in 1981, 1982, 1983, 1988, 1989
This Angus & Robertson Bluegum edition published in 1991
Reprinted in 1993, 1996, 2001, 2002
by HarperCollins*Publishers* Pty Limited
ABN 36 009 913 517
A member of the HarperCollins*Publishers* (Australia) Pty Limited Group
www.harpercollins.com.au

HarperCollins*Publishers*
25 Ryde Road, Pymble, Sydney NSW 2073, Australia
31 View Road, Glenfield, Auckland 10, New Zealand
77–85 Fulham Palace Road, London W6 8JB, United Kingdom
Hazelton Lanes, 55 Avenue Road, Suite 2900, Toronto, Ontario, M5R 3L2
and 1995 Markham Road, Scarborough, Ontario, M1B 5M8, Canada
10 East 53rd Street, New York NY 10022, USA

National Library of Australia Cataloguing-in-Publication data:

Paterson, A. B. (Andrew Barton), 1864–1941.
Mulga Bill's bicycle.
ISBN 0 207 17284 6.
1. Bicycles – Juvenile poetry. 2. Children's poetry, Australian.
I. Niland, Kilmeny. II. Niland, Deborah. III. Title.
A821'.2

Typeset by Computype, Sydney
Printed in Hong Kong by Printing Express on 128gsm Matt Art

14 13 12 11   02 03 04 05

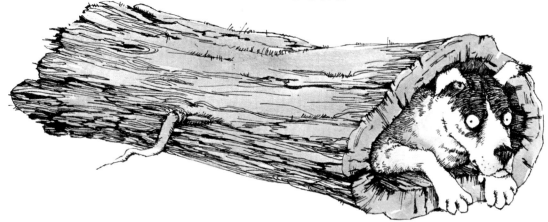

'Twas Mulga Bill, from Eaglehawk,
that caught the cycling craze;

He turned away the good old horse that served him many days;

He dressed himself in cycling clothes, resplendent to be seen;
He hurried off to town and bought a shining new machine;

And as he wheeled it through the door,
                with air of lordly pride,
The grinning shop assistant said,
                "Excuse me, can you ride?"

"See here, young man," said Mulga Bill, "from Walgett to the sea,
From Conroy's Gap to Castlereagh, there's none can ride like me.

I'm good all round at everything, as everybody knows,
Although I'm not the one to talk—I hate a man that blows.

"But riding is my special gift, my chiefest, sole delight;
Just ask a wild duck can it swim, a wild cat can it fight.
There's nothing clothed in hair or hide, or built of flesh or steel,
There's nothing walks or jumps, or runs, on axle, hoof, or wheel,
But what I'll sit, while hide will hold and girths and straps are tight;
I'll ride this here two-wheeled concern right straight away at sight."

'Twas Mulga Bill, from Eaglehawk, that sought his own abode,
That perched above the Dead Man's Creek, beside the mountain road.

He turned the cycle down the hill and mounted for the fray,
But ere he'd gone a dozen yards it bolted clean away.

It left the track, and through the trees, just like a silver streak,
It whistled down the awful slope towards the Dead Man's Creek.

It shaved a stump by half an inch,

it dodged a big white-box:

The very wallaroos in fright went scrambling up the rocks,

The wombats hiding in their caves dug deeper underground,

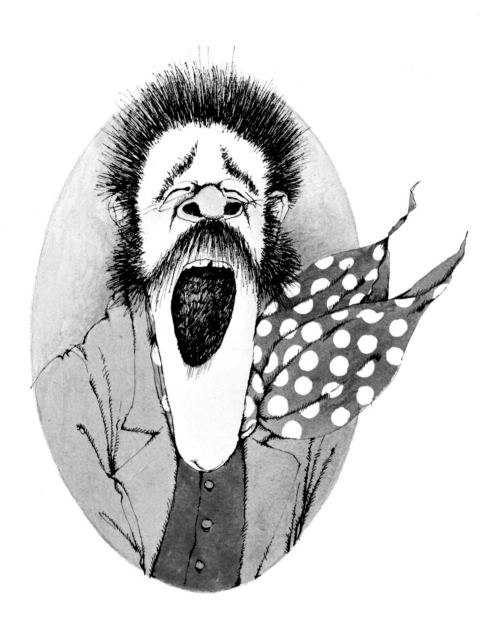

But Mulga Bill, as white as chalk, sat tight to every bound.

It struck a stone and gave a spring
that cleared a fallen tree,

It raced beside a precipice as close as close could be;

And then, as Mulga Bill let out one last despairing shriek,

It made a leap of twenty feet into the Dead Man's Creek.

'Twas Mulga Bill, from Eaglehawk, that slowly swam ashore:
He said, "I've had some narrer shaves and lively rides before;
I've rode a wild bull round a yard to win a five-pound bet,
But this was sure the derndest ride that I've encountered yet.
I'll give that two-wheeled outlaw best; it's shaken all my nerve
To feel it whistle through the air and plunge and buck and swerve,

It's safe at rest in Dead Man's Creek—we'll leave it lying still;
A horse's back is good enough henceforth for Mulga Bill."